Destined for Greatness

A book of poetry, inspirational thoughts and prayers

When travelling your road to greatness
you may seem alone
but God has assigned an angel
Jus to take you through
so don't give up
And never give in.
J.Y.W. 26/10/15

Copyright © 2018 Janet Y. Williams

All Rights Reserved

Well here's to living life to the fullest each and every day. May the love, joy and peace be forever my friends. Love you all. May you all be forever blessed and loved.

Janet Y. Williams
4th December 2015

The Serenity Prayer (partial)

God grant me the SERENITY to accept the things I cannot change, the COURAGE to change the things I can, and the WISDOM to know the difference.

This book is dedicated to the memories of my mother, Eva M. Ferguson-Williams, my brother, Sgt. 1578 Kevin P.A. Williams and my sister, Christine I.L. Williams-Dillet. But especially to my living support team, my kids, Tristan, Matthew, Ava, Janeva and Ian. Thanks for all the love guys. Mama loves you all.

Acknowledgement

Can't believe I am actually doing this. I have been challenged by a few friends and my two oldest children, to put pen to paper. To put my poetry and writings in a book to be published. I have accepted this challenge whole heartedly. I pray that at the end of it all, I can inspire others to follow their dreams and hearts' desires. To set their goals and standards high. To find and fulfil their purpose. And to finish everything they started. Let my words challenge you to be conquerors. Conquerors for God. Conquerors of negativity. Conquerors of evil. Accomplishers of goals. Accomplishers of dreams. Be the great achievers God has designed us all to be. This I challenge myself and you all to do this and more. Be great for greatness is in you all.

Life, Love, Happiness and Inner Peace

Life is always how you make it.
Life can transition from your
Dreams to your realities.
Life is and always will be
More than you expect or anticipate.

Love stems from life lessons.
For without love you have no life.
Love makes life worth living
Or your life would be meaningless
Love and life co-exist to have
Happiness.

Happiness is a product of
The love and life combination.
Happiness is in-explainable in words
But an emotion that adds to us
All as we try to live better lives.
With the enhancement of life and love
Happiness comes and produces
Inner Peace.

Inner Peace comes from
A better life
More love
And a happiness of mind and soul.
Inner Peace was given to us by God.
But, we as humans get caught up in
Earthly possessions,
Love of self (arrogance),
Love of things,
Happiness of man's form of love.

But, you find your
Inner Peace when you find
God's love that is unconditional,
God's joy that cannot be measured,
God's peace that even though storms
Are raging around you,
You can stand still,

Look up,
Smile
And know that you are
One with self
One with soul
One with spirit
And most importantly
One with God.

Live life to the fullest
Knowing that
Love will find you
Ready for the
Happiness that will come from
Having a God who will guide you to
Your Inner Peace.

As I have gotten older, I have also become wiser. I remember being called many things but especially a cold hearted bitch. But with so many labels like being a lesbian, being a whore, to name a few, I have realized that they all made me stronger and I remember my mom's words, "Show them better than you can tell them." I have had terrible dark days when I wanted to end my life, and I have the physical scars to remind me about those dark days. I remember my days of making dumb and stupid decisions. But I have gained strength from every bad relationship. Every bad situation because when the good came they were great and long lasting. I believe in lifting up others no matter how dark my mood, my day or how bad my situation may be. Because by doing that I help me heal even more. Over the years I still have those moments when I want to end it all but God steps in and shows me that I am great. I am awesome. I am loved and blessed. I pass this on today to help someone either help themselves or to help someone else they may know. Pass on a smile. Pass on a kind word. Pass on agape love to all, especially your enemies. Love, peace, happiness is yours to have, share and receive.
#findyourpurposeloveyouaboveearthlygain#.

Why Waste Time

Why waste time
When you can be
Bold and express
How and what you
Truly feel for someone.

Why waste time
With people
Who mean you no good
And waste your
Time, love and life.

Why waste time
When you can
Be happy
Feel love
And have peace in your life.

Why waste time
When life is
So short
And your days
And numbered.

Why waste time
When you have
So little to waste
When you can fill
It with needs and wants.

Why waste time
And your youth on
People whether
Family, friends or lovers,
When there is someone
Out there who will
Give you all you
Can ever want, need or desire.
So to all those
I know and love
Why go through
Life doing what makes

Us unhappy and unsatisfied
So my beloveds
Why waste time.

Greatness is not something we are born with; it is something we evolve ourselves into. Greatness isn't something given by man but transferred from God. To be great you have to ask for God's guidance and a spirit of discernment. To be great you have to let go of people, things and bad habits. To be great reduce your inner circle. Strengthen your inner man. Love and respect God, yourself and others. To be great, motivate others, never let it be all about you. Peace. Happiness. Love and greatness are ours to create, to achieve, to share and to show to all. #begreatnomatterwhat#

Love

Love
A word many use
And never sincerely mean.

Love
A word that is more
Than an expression of emotion.

Love
A word that can be
Expressed, felt and shown.

Love
A word that is either
Shown physically or by actions.

Love
A word that can
Create a life or destroy many.

Love
When sincerely shown
Builds, strengthens, protects
And guides us all
Down a path to
Unexpected joys
Unexpected pleasures
Unexpected dreams
Unexpected happiness.

Love
Shared with all
Expressed by few
Created by many
And spread endlessly.

Wow can't believe it's been 14 years since my only brother unsolved murder, but I pushed pass the pain, the tears, the hurt, the unknowing of who and why, to remember the laughs, the dances, the counselling moments, the talks about dating and boys. The days of him teaching me how to drive stick shift and our crazy moments of late night eating and watching creature feature horror classics. As I look back on my life I have limited regrets. And as I look forward and see more happiness. More love. More positivity. More God and more time for my kids, family and close circle friends. I thank God for everything and everyone that He has placed in my life because for ever bad, I have received good. For every hurt I have received joy. And for every brokenness I have been healed. I thank God for my children because without them I would have no reason to push pass everything and they help me stay focused. I say all of that to say this, no matter how dark the days, that there is still hope for a bigger, better and brighter future. God places trials and challenges in our lives to strengthen, encourage and bring us closer to Him. So as we go through our daily lives, pass on love. Pass on encouragement. And be your brothers' and sisters' keepers. Let go of all the bad things that people have done to you, so that you can live and walk in God's peace. Forever surrounded by the beauty that it offers. So today I encourage you all to be a pillar of strength, love and hope if only for one other person than yourself. May God's peace, love and understanding surround your hearts always.

Blessed and Devoted

Blessed
Because you are
A blessing to my life.

Devoted
Because you have
Devoted yourself to being my friend.

Blessed and Blunt
Earnestly honest
Respectful of others
Never scared
Arousing of greatness
Raising the bar higher
Devoted to family and true friends.

Daily walking with God
Admirable in character
Visionary in your unique way
Intelligence beyond body
Sexy and sensual as hell.
You will always be
Eye-candy
My best friend
My forever love
My blessing
My devotion.

Much love, respect and honour to you all my peeps. It amazes me that so many of us search for a mate, and in some cases never get it right straight out the gate. But for those who have a great guy in your life support him. Pull his greatness out of him. When he is having a bad day, be the peace and sanctuary he needs at the end of that day. And guys who have a great girl, who doing her thing but still supports you in your dream, hold on tight because if one of "ya boys" wishes she was theirs. Yes, it is great to be an independent guy or girl, but at the same time be dependent on that one person, who loves you through your flaws. Holds your hand just for the heck of it. Who feels your pain when you cry? And who says you can when everybody else tells you that you can't. To my INDEPENDENT ladies, yeah the career is good. The materials are nice, but what happens when the kids are grown and gone and there is no one left to share your life with. And to my REAL men who striving for greatness because you never know who watching and who God has designed just for you, keep moving in a positive way. Women please never look down on a guy who has to break a date or two, because he trying to get somewhere in life without being a thug. And guys just because she pushes as hard as you do, don't mean she doesn't want, desire or need you to love, cherish and protect her. Work hard. Play hard. And live and love life to the fullest. And never settle for less than you deserve. I love you all in different ways. Peace. Happiness. Joy and love are all yours. Grab life by the horns and live it. Day in. Day out.

My Wow Factor

Wow is the best way
To describe how I feel
Whenever we talk.

Wow is what I say
To myself
Just knowing i now have you.

Wow is how you
Make me feel
Knowing that you have my back.

All I can say
After every conversation with
You eye-candy is
Wow.

Wow as another birthday approaches, I am remembering all our conversations. All the advice given. I never realized that our last four years together would be our best. Really need you but you left me with everything I need to carry on with. Really miss you mummy. For those who still have someone, who means them well. Give you wise and good advice. Shows you love when everybody else turns away. Show them how much they mean to you because you never when God will move them out of your life. Show love even to those who do you wrong. Live your life each day with a smile on your lips. A song in your heart. And wisdom and success in all you do. Be blessed so that you can be a blessing. Because as I sit in my room with a heavy heart, but yet a light one, remembering the great, little woman that my mother was and praying that I can and will be if only half as great as she was. I say do great things every day by the little things you do, without looking for earthly recognition. I love each and every one of you. Stay blessed. Stay focused. Stay loved. Make peace and joy forever follow you all.

The Total Package

Everybody searching.
Their total package
Must be this
Or must be that.
Please God send him or her
With a fine body
A fine face
Curly or straight hair
Tall with pretty eyes and teeth.
But, what about
Do they have
A kind and giving heart
Does their soul dwell in peace?
Do they spread love and peace?
Instead of hate and anger
Does their eyes
See all the great and good creations
Does their lips
Spread the words of love and joy
As a temple where God dwells
Does their spiritual being
Live and love God firstly
Do their ears
Hear all the positive and great thing
Does their lives
Prove how awesome our God is
Most importantly do they walk
Daily with God as their guide
This to me is
The Total Package.

We sometimes get disappointed in life but I remember my mummy used to say, "Disappointments does be for the best." So even though they come I appreciate them and learn and move on. So even when you get disappointed look at the advantages given because of them. #lovingmydisppointments#

The Future

The future
Holds mysteries yet unknown
And yet to be experienced.

The future
Holds untold stories
Of love, pains, sorrows and joys.

The future
Holds gifts and blessings
Unseen and waiting.

The future
Is what you make
And want it to be.

The future
Is yet ahead to
Make, create and experience.

The future
Is filled with dreams, goals and achievements
Yet to be done.

What will you want
Need
Desire
And yearn for
The Future.

I am at that point in my life where I getting rid of baggage. Garbage and people who don't deserve to have me in their life. Nor are they worth my time and effort to get to know. As my forty plus birthday is just a little way away I am making my circle smaller and tighter. Like my mummy always said, "I checking for who checking for me." You each had or may still have a place in my life. But if you no longer receive messages and texts from me, it only means that you have been deleted. Love you all at some point for different reasons. But I heading into my selfish season, where I have to love me. Care about me. Take care of me and focus on my happiness and not the happiness of others. Tired giving all and receiving crap back. I am done and moving on. Good bye and good riddance, I say to what I no longer love. No longer live for. No longer need. Doing me and what makes me happy. And like my bff said, "Time to make myself available to change." To new adventures. New hope. New life. New love. It has truly been great but I must move on for my own sanity. Peace out. And to my new friends, I say thank you for its time for me to do everything differently.

Always Thinking Of You

I never would have imagined and
Don't know why
But you travel through my mind
Almost every second of every day
Because I am
Always thinking of you.

Every time we talk
I learn something new
Whether it is something we have in common
Or something that is unique about you
So I will
Always be thinking about you.

With each passing day
I know I fall deeper
And more in love with you
Because we have connected like no other
On levels I thought were no longer there
And this is why I am
Always thinking about you.

It amazes me that after years of dating and having someone in my life as a significant other, I have now been single for over two years. I am amazed that guys that once fascinated me, no longer interest me. And now that I am no longer looking to date or even be in a relationship all these guys, younger, my age and older now find me interesting. But such is life. I will continue to do me and my kids until God sends my ONE. All I can and will say to those who are single, do you. Fix you. Love you. Live your life to the fullest and enjoy each day. Each second. Each moment and make loving and lasting memories.
#doingmelovingmefixingme#

Courageous Enduring Friend

Courageous and bold
Enduring and extraordinary
Friend to the end and fabulous.

You stand out from
The rest because of your
Uniqueness
Understanding
Loveable
Admirable
Caring
Sensual
And overwhelming
Heart a lifetime of happiness
Joy, love and peace with you
All I have to say is that
I have fallen and can't and don't
Understand nor care why
For you
And all I have left to say is
I Love You.

As I get older, I get bored faster. It amazes how things and people that once fascinated me no longer do. Now I know I am getting older and wiser because my circle of friends is shrinking. My search for earthly love has ended because I am seeking a higher and greater love that any earthly person can or even try to give. My search to find me is over because I have me. Love the woman I am, and those who for and with me will receive the benefits of being there with and for me. So for those searching for who and what you think you cannot find look within and trust me, your search will end.

Fell For You And You Didn't Know

Wow,
I can't believe
That after all the brokenness
Through all the trials
From all the bad breaks
After all the terrible decisions
I believe I have finally
Gotten it right
I pray daily that my past
Mistakes and decisions
Help strengthen and wizen me
So that I won't do them again
As I get older
I have grown wiser
And have learned that while
The package may look good
Smell good
Taste and feel good
That it may not be good
For me
But now I look beyond
All of that to the heart
Which is the most important
And I have found a heart like mine
And I am blessed
To know that finally
Things are turning around
You have shown how much better
My tomorrows can be
If I embrace
My today
So while you may have
A struggle
A hard time getting through to me
That I have already
Fallen for you and you didn't know.

As my next birthday fastly approaches I am grateful and thankful for family and friends, who have stuck by me through all my craziness. Bad moments. Sad moments. Moments of joy and pleasure. Held my hand through the deaths of my mom, sister and only brother. Thankful for every hard and tough time because they made me wiser, stronger and more loved. I can say that even though things may be a bit rough I can and will move boldly forward with a smile on my lips and a song in my heart. To those who said I couldn't and wouldn't make it, I laugh and say, "I still living, loving and moving forever forward." Thanks for the hurtful and mean words because they built me up even stronger. I say to you all who are reading this that no matter what people and society say who you are, doesn't matter because of who God made you to be that counts. I love each of you differently and thank God daily for you. All I ask is that you strive for God's purpose and perfection of who you are designed to be. Be happy and seek peace in your life's choices/ to my closest friends, I love you ever so dearly and you need not worry about me, I gonna be ever so much better and happier. To my kids, mama loves you greatly and differently. To those who fear me keep it up because God has bigger, better and brighter for me. And to you all keep pushing forward with no hate and no regrets.

Give Thanks Always

No matter the day
No matter the hour
No matter the circumstances
Especially at your darkest hour
Remember to
Give thanks always.

Because where there is life
There is hope
Where there is hope
There is faith
Where there is faith
There you will find God, so
Give thanks always.

Because while you complaining
Someone is praising
While you cursing man and God
Someone is thanking God
And while you crying
God is calling on you to
Give thanks always.

Because when you think
You have it bad
The person you complaining to
Has it a whole lot worse
But they smile and encourage you
To give thanks always.

As I got up this gorgeous morning I have realized that my trials. My hard times. My heartaches. My headaches all came so that I can learn. Grow. Gain wisdom. Gain knowledge. Gain peace. Find me. Find hope. Find my faith. Most importantly find God. I have seeked things and people for years for these and had them all along travelling with and inside of me. Those who are a part of my inner circle know of just some of my demons and struggles, but not all of them. As I sit, I count my blessings. I look back on what I thought were lost opportunities, but what turned out to be life lessons and movements in greatness. As I look at where I am now heading, I am happy for my struggles. Happy for my trials. Happy for my heartaches. Happy for past mistakes. For they all set me up for greatness. Set me up for where I need to go. Set me up for the woman, mother, friend, lover and person that I need to be. Set me up for who God has made me to be. For my haters out there keep hating, cause your hateration will continue to be my motivation. Greatness in me that is now shining through all the darken corners of my life. To my kids, wow I am proud to be called your mother. I love each of you differently. To my family, let us pull together and make each other great. To my closest friends, thanks because there were days I couldn't make it without you pushing me. To my new friends, let's keep in contact and help each other even if only with a kind and loving word. I challenge each of you to pull the great men and women that God has designed each of us to be, out and let your lights drive and brighten every dark corner in this world and make your enemies run and hide. Live. Love. Share peace. And most importantly show Agape Love, the love of God, especially to your enemies and those who think you aren't great.

New Breath

I now have new breath
I now have new life
I now have new outlook
I now have new faith
I now have new love
I now have new hope
I now have new dreams
I now have new goals
I now have new achievements
I now have new days
And with all this newness
I now will be able
To do all things new
Being renewed
Refreshed
Revised
Revived
Reloved
Reinvented
I can and will
Do more
Do bigger
Do greater
With each new day
Brings everything new
New love
New hope
New faith
New walk
New talk
New smile
New joy
New breath.

Hey world are you ready, for another great person to accomplish their dreams. Their goals. Their aspirations. Hey world are you ready, for someone to use their God given talents to inspire others to achieve their greatness. I hope you are because that's how it it's going to be. As you each start your day look up and say thanks to our Heavenly Father, because you are still here to make corrections. Accomplish dreams. Seek forgiveness. Forgive others and show Agape love. No matter what you may be going through just know the God we serve has greatness in store for ALL of us. Remember to smile because you are loved and cherished by God and many.

I Have To Love, Me

How can I show love?
If I don't love me
How can I be better?
If I don't love me
How can I encourage
If I don't love me
How can I live
If I don't love me
How can I move on?
If I don't love me
How can I be happy?
If I don't love me
How can I love you?
If I don't love me
So to do all these things
I have to love, me.

As I live my life, I have seen pain, sorrow, hurt, emptiness, abandonment and heartlessness, but I have come to the realization that every bad experience, every terrible situation and every ugly thing that we pass through in life there is always something great, beautiful and unexpected that can and will be learned if we open our minds, our hearts and our eyes to find the beauty that surrounds us. Sometimes it takes something bad to let us know that something or someone better is out there just waiting for our bad times to end, to create our great things begin. So I challenge each of you to always look beyond tour bad to days for your bigger, better and brighter tomorrows. Look for the inner peace of God to encompass you as you go through bad times. Look for the love of family and real friends to help you get over your sorrows. Look to God to pull you through when you think you can't go on. And look to self and your heart to see what God has placed in front of you and within your reach. Learn that, "Yes it might be rough now but my bigger, better ad brighter is coming." Know that for every bad relationship there is one that will bring you true joy, true peace, true happiness and a never ending supply of love. For God has designed a perfect soul-mate, lifetime partner, best friend and guidance counsellor for each of us. As you embark on a new week, may it bring you all closer to finding what and who you need to add to you and may you also find the courage to get over your fears, doubts, discouragements and past to all the beautiful and great things and people that are either already in your life nor who will come. Pray to get over your past so that all your tomorrows and will be the best ones you have ever seen. May love, faith, peace, hope and joy carry you through your hard times and bring you out better than you were before.

Just Cause

J. C.
Just Cause
You think you ugly
Don't mean we do

J.C.
Just Cause
You drink and party a lot
Means you are an alcoholic and party animal.

J.C.
Just Cause
You think you a sex beast
Means that we believe.

J.C.
Just Cause
You are you
And what you believe in
And what you strive for
Makes you awesome in
Your own way.

J.C.
Just Cause
We love you
Because you are
Just Cool
Just Crazy
Just uncontrollable
Just Courageous.

As we travel through life, we have to learn when to let go and when to fight for what and who we need and want in our lives. We sometimes make the mistake of letting go when we should hold on. And holding on when we should let go. But if you feel great with whatever decision you have made, then you know you made the right one. Love comes in all shapes, sizes, ages, groups and sex, but if it is genuine hold on to it and enjoy it for as long as you have it. So I challenge you all today to fight for who you need and want in your life, because it is too short to have regrets.

My Eyes Are Open

My eyes are open
To the beauty that surrounds me
To the blessings I now have
To the blessings that are coming
To a love like none I have ever known
To new hopes to enjoy
To new joy to spread
To new dreams and goals to achieve
To bigger, brighter, greater future.

My eyes are open
To a darkened past
To a scarred heart
To brokenness
To sleepless nights
To negativity and negative people
To toxic relationships
To the loss of things and people.

Thank you God
For all you have done
And continue to do
But finally helping me to
Open my eyes.

As we embark on a new season in a matter of hours, may we all look at past blessings. Past mistakes to be corrected. Dreams to be achieved. Goals to be set and accomplished. Love to seek and find. Wisdom to be gained. With the new season close upon us, let us reflect on what we need and what need to do. Let us take a retrospective look at the lives we have led and the ones we want to and need to lead. May those who are in search of whatever it may be, I pray you find it and that it enriches your lives. Let us all strive for greatness and positive changes. May you who seek love find an abundance of it. Those seeking better living and jobs, I pray you obtain them. Let us continuously be our brothers' ad sisters' keepers, that way we have better neighborhoods. Better society. And I love you all in different ways for you each fulfil a different purpose in my life.

Have You Looked In The Mirror

Have you looked in the mirror?
And smiled at the person you see
Knowing the love, they have to give away.

Have you looked in the mirror?
And loved the person looking back at you
Knowing that they are truly worthy of love.

Have you looked in the mirror?
And see the strength that is within
The face staring back.

Have you looked in the mirror and see?
All of the things you wanted
For yourself.

Look in the mirror
Smile, love, cherish and appreciate
New life, new love, new beginnings
For greatness is coming.

To all my Bahamian people out there, continue to be encouraged. Look to our Heavenly Father for the strength you need to walk away from a problem. Stop being negative statistics and start being the solutions. Keep Psalms 91 close to you always, for it will help you get where you need to be. Much blessings on you all. Pray for me as I continue to pray for you all.

Dear Matthew

To my second oldest son
May you come to know the full realization
Of how awesome and great you are
May you know that God will
Forever watch over, guide and protect you
May you value yourself
And stand up for what you believe
And know to be right
May you follow the path
That God has set before you
May you always know
How loved and blessed you are
And may you let God
Guide your actions and words
May opportunities continue
To run you down
May love dwell
Forever in your heart
May peace dwell
Forever in your life
May happiness dwell
In your thoughts
May wisdom
Always fall from your lips
And may God's peace
Be how you live your life.

Happy sweet sixteenth.

As we moved forward in life and moving boldly forward to new life, let us
look at what we accomplished in the past and make corrections and adjustments in the years to come. Always show God's love, share His peace and encourage others to better themselves. For when you do this you not only make someone's day or make them smile, but you also gladden your own heart. Because when you do this you actually forget your worries and stresses and allow God to change you and others for the better. With every new day that you are given, be a light of love and hope to this world while you are here. Live. Love and share a word of blessing and encouragement to all you encounter. Love you all and be a blessing to those around you.

Joyous Occasions

For everything that happens in your life
That causes you to celebrate are
Joyous occasions.

For all the small and great blessings
That God sends your way to show are
Joyous occasions.

For just waking up with a home
Family, friends and life are
For the ability to praise God are
Joyous occasions.

For the ability to praise God
And be in your right mind are
Joyous occasions.

For the gifts of happiness, joy and kindness
And to share these with others are
Joyous occasions.

For the abilities to walk, talk and
Share the words of God are
Joyous occasions.

Share a kind word
Share some love
Share a word of encouragement
Show agape love
Show kindness
Show genuine care
Be your brothers' and sisters' keepers
Be a pillar of strength
For once you can do all
These you add to yourself
And to society
And you make the world
A brighter, happier and better place
For sharing is the greatest part of
Joyous Occasions.

To all the strong women I know, whether you gave birth to a child/children or you are blessed with being a mentor to children. Your job is a never ending one. With no time outs. No vacations and no pay. Some days you don't even get a thank you for all you do. Being a mother I is a blessed job and one of the best that you can and ever will have. For those of us who are mothers and still have your mothers in your lives, look up and thank God for her. For without her, not only wouldn't you be here, but your greatness would still be hidden. There are days I wish mine was still here if only for one last conversation. But I thank God for my time with her. Share your love, your laughter, your heartaches and pains and joys not just with your children but with your children, but with others that will pass across your paths. Encourage and enrich the lives of others with a mother's love.

Feeling Brand New

Feeling brand new
Because it's a
Brand new day
Filled with new
Hopes of a better life
Faith that tomorrow will be greater
Love that will conquer all fears
Dreams that will become realities
Goals set that will be accomplished
Happiness sort after that will be found
Joys seeked and found
Lifetime partners so long searched for that com at the right time
Brand new is starting every day afresh
Brand new life
Brand new hopes
Brand new dreams
Brand new happiness
Brand new joys
Brand new loves
And most importantly
A brand new you
So every day wake up
Feeling brand new.

Everybody searching for the next best thing. Their Mr. or Miss Right. That quick fix to a broken heart. Well I say search within. Make your changes. Make sure you are happy with who you are. Become the person you want to date, love and share a lifetime with. Because when you single you have time to fix you. You have the time to love you. You have the time to search deep within and look, make and see your mistakes. When you are single you have time for God, yourself and your family. But when you are in a committed relationship, whether it be intimate or just friends, you have to work. Work to keep it spicy. Work to keep it growing. Work to help it flourish. Work to keep it loving and lasting. Many people give advice on what a good relationship is. But at the end of the day we each know and feel what relationships work for us and those that work against us. If you woke up each day with a smile on your lips and a song in your heart that's part of being in a great relationship. If you find yourself with butterflies, with the anticipation of seeing her or him, that's the beginning of a good relationship. If you find yourself can't sleep because you have not spoken to them that is yet another sign of a good relationship. Also if you see you can't rest or find peace because you had an argument and you aren't willing to let them go because you want and need them, then you on the right path. Someone once said, "True love is about commitment." But it isn't, it's first about honesty. Then communication. But real, true and sincere love starts from within. And every strong, solid and lasting intimate relationship must and I stress must be headed by God. Cause if He isn't in the picture it won't last. In everyone's life, you will have bad experiences. Please use them to learn what works and doesn't work for you. And let go when your heart, soul and mind agrees that you aren't happy with who you with, and for those, who like me, still looking don't get into anything you aren't willing to keep, hold on to or fight for, and make sure they feel the same about you. An old man once told me, "It's good for a man to be a woman's first love, but better for a woman to be a man's last love." And that right there is what we all want. To be a person's last love, because when you are their last and they are yours, therefore there is no desire, need nor want to go looking for anyone else for anything. Love is yours to obtain. Now go out there and get it, and guys and gals, please stop using others as a jump off point, quick fixes and sex buddies because you, to will be the ones hurting in the end. Always show Agape Love, which is the love of God, to others especially your enemies.

Life's Real Pleasures

Our search is always ongoing
We search for earthly treasures
We search for earthly love

We search for earthly possessions
We search for the tangible things
We search for the love of man
We search for society's pleasure
We always searching but never finding
We always searching and already have
We always searching for what we think we need
We always searching for what we want
We always searching for nothing of great value
We always searching for man
And not for God
While we searching
We losing out on what we have
We losing out on what we really need
We losing out on true happiness
We losing out on true love
We losing out on truly living
We losing out on our blessings
We losing out on all that God has for us
Time to stop searching
Time to stop losing out
Time to start loving
Time to start living
Most importantly time to
Seek God and all of
Life's real pleasures and treasures
Treasure joy
Treasure love
Treasure inner peace
Treasure happiness
And treasure God's richest blessings
For those are all
Life's real pleasures.

It just amazes me how people judge you based on the opinion of one Whether this person be family, friend or foe. I was taught to always get both sides before I make a decision on how to treat and know a person. Because the person coming to you, like we say 'toting news' especially bad news about someone, is jealous, envious, hateful and casting their shadow over that person's life. The Father says, "judge not lest you be judged." You nor they have walked in that person's shoes, nor living their life. You never know what a person faces when they don't complain. We, many times, take the opinion of one to cast blame and judgment on another. If you can't lift a person up, don't talk about them, because what you may say about them shows the world who you truly are. I am happy in the skin I am in, and thank God daily for my blessings. Persons have called me delusional, but yet they come to me with their problems. Persons have called me a beggar, but yet asks me for stuff and to do for them. Persons have lied on me and called me a liar I waste not my time any more getting angry or passing judgment on others. I use my time wisely, by praying for God to bless them and move them out my way, so that I can and will do what He has for me to do. It's time for us to stop casting blame and judgment on another. Because, you don't know their story and you have not walked in their shoes. So when powerful be very humble, because the God that may have blessed you yesterday will be the very same one to elevate and bless the person whose name you just talked about. I love my life and ONLY God can judge me. Yes, I have made mistakes and I have learned from them and won't let my children make the same ones. So before you take sides find out the full story. Bless them that curse you and watch God open flood gates of blessings for you and your future generations. Never concern yourself about how bad someone talks about you, just think how God will bless you. They talked about Christ, so are we. If you taking time out your busy schedule to talk about me, then I am more important to you than what you have to do for yourself.

Move On

Never thought it would come to this
Never thought it would have ended
Never thought I would be heartbroken, again
Never thought of starting over once more
Never thought I would have to let go
Never thought my tears would fall
Never thought my fears would be reality
Never thought you would not be there
Never thought you would give up
Never thought you would hurt again
Never thought you would fall weak
Never thought the love would stop
Never thought the goodness would end
Never thought our lives would change
But here we are
Letting go of each other
Letting what we thought we had, end
Letting go of what was special
Letting go may not feel good
Letting go may not feel right
Letting go may hurt
But we have decided to
Move on
Move away
Move apart
Move forward single
But moving on
Is what we must do
What we need to d
What we have to do
To heal
To grow
To love
To live
Moving on
Is best for us both
For us to be happy
We must sadly
Move on.

How many of us have given thanks for or reflected on the great sacrifice that was made for us by Christ? How many of us would make any sacrifice for the sake of others? How many of us would give up something we love for the benefit of mankind? As simple as a meal to give a family that has nothing to be given in return. Many may say, "yes I will," but in their hearts, they know they never will. It goes far beyond praying for others and blessing others like Christ did for us thousands of years ago. He gave up His freedom and life so that we can find our way to God. How many are willing to do the same if only for their loved ones? Very, very few and sadly before we bless others with a kind word or a word of encouragement, we drag them down. Instead of building up someone, we prefer to degrade and destroy them. So to you, my family, friends and loved ones let's be builders and not destroyers, not just to each other, but to anyone you encounter as you pass through life's journey. Because, the person you build today, may be a blessing to you tomorrow. So let us share our lives and love with those around us.

Forever Thankful

God has given you
A new day
For a new blessing
So that you can be
Forever thankful.

God has given you
A new hope
For bigger and better
Things to come so be
Forever thankful

God has given you
A new dream
To create a better world
So that we can be
Forever thankful

God has given you
A new song
To play when times get rough
So that you can be
Forever thankful

God has given you
A new walk
So that He will direct your steps
So that you can be
Forever thankful.

God has given you
A new talk
So that you can spread His word
So that the world can be
Forever thankful

God has given you
A new faith
To pull you closer to Him
So that you can be
Forever thankful

God has given you
His peace
That surpasses all understanding
So that you can be
Forever thankful.

We have so much
To look forward to
To gain
To grow for
To live for
To love more
So be forever thankful.

For hard times
For trials
For tests
For family
For friends
For loved ones
For enemies
Because we need good and bad
So that we can be
Forever Thankful.

Ok here's the thing. How many of us around the forty and above age bracket have reached the tired and fed up point? Well, I have. Now that I am making all the right and positive changes to my life, some are beyond pissed. But you know what, I honestly don't care how they feel because I doing what is best for me and my kids! And to those who don't like me. Well I say to you move the hell on. I am going to do everything I always wanted to do for myself, my family and very few friends. Happier that my circle is getting smaller. That way I know who truly love and care for me. And to my haters, please keep hating. Because you see, you are truly my motivators in a big way. Love to those who keep pushing me to strive to achieve my dreams and goals. And for those who say they love me, time to prove it. Stop talking and start doing, because I am so done with the talkers.

Crossroads

As you get older
And you gain more knowledge
And experience what life has to offer
You will always come
To major or minor
Crossroads.

As you live each moment
And more from day to day learn something new
Have at least one new experience
Because you will come to
Crossroads.

These crossroads
Will help you
Gain experience
Gain knowledge
Gain wisdom
To move on to more
Crossroads.

These crossroads
Adds more value
More love
More life
So that you will look forward to your
Crossroads.

Enjoy your crossroads
Love your crossroads
Find peace in your crossroads
Learn from your crossroads
Because you will have them
And you need
Crossroads.

Amazing Prayers for Amazing People

To all my family and friends, at this joyous season may you all remember why we celebrate the birth of our Lord and Savior. May you all be blessed, safe and have inner peace, knowing that you have a protective covering over you. May the upcoming year be better, more fulfilling, more blessed, more productive and filled with the love of God, family and true friends. May all your dreams come to floriation ad bring you and those around you utter joy. May God's angels watch over and keep you all safe during this Holy season. May the mistakes, heartaches, heartbreaks and pains be n more in the year to come. For those living unhappily, my prayer is that as this year rolls out, so does all your problems. And that in the new year all start a fresh with renewed spirit, mind, body and soul. Stay safe and blessed my family and ley God's will be done in your life from this day forward. Peace, love and happiness, I pray over your lives in the years to come. Amen

To all my family and friends, may the love of God forever be in your lives. May you always pass on a kind word or a word of encouragement just to help someone to have a brighter outlook. Pass on love today because you never know who will be called home. But most importantly love sincerely and open heartedly, because you never know who is meant to stay a part of your life. Amen

For all the men out there who deserve the title of Father, I pray that God continually bless, guide and protect you. For those of you who just help with the conception and leave, please consider the fact that one day the children you discard will become great men and women of this grand nation. For the cornerstone the builder rejected God will make the head cornerstone. And my brother out there, if it doesn't work out between you and your children's mother, please do not use you children as pawns in some sick twisted game. Because at the end of the day you will be the ones to lose out. To my friends out there who grew up with just mummy, be better men, fathers and builders of this nation that we are blessed to be in. let this all be done through God and let His will be done in your lives. Amen

Father, I ask in the name of your son, Jesus Christ, to bless, guide and protect all my family and friends. Father I ask that no matter what they going through to give, you, God all the thanks and the praise and the glory. That your will be done in their lives and mine. Amen.

Made in the USA
Columbia, SC
13 October 2024

43501450R00035